D0100271

THE THREE WISHES

by
Charles Perrault

Illustrated by
Meredith Lightbown

Troll Associates

Copyright © 1979 by Troll Associates
All rights reserved. No part of this book may be used or reproduced
in any manner whatsoever without written permission from the publisher.
Printed in the United States of America.

Troll Associates, Mahwah, N.J.

Library of Congress Catalog Card Number: 78-18060
ISBN 0-89375-129-4

Once upon a time, long, long ago, there was a very poor woodsman. He lived with his wife in a tiny cottage at the edge of the woods. Every day, he went into the forest and cut down trees with his ax. He worked all day long, and he worked very hard.

"Work, work, work," he said, as he swung his ax. "Someday I will not have to work so hard. Someday I will have a big house and plenty of food. Someday I will be rich!" But no matter how many trees he cut down, he remained just as poor as ever.

One day, when he was deep in the forest, he came to a huge oak tree. He thought about all the lumber he could get from such a tree. And he made up his mind to cut it down, no matter how long it might take. He picked up his ax and was about to swing it, when he heard a voice behind him.

"Stop!" cried the voice.

The woodsman was so startled that he dropped his ax. And when he turned around, he could hardly believe his eyes. There, right before him, stood a tree fairy.

"This tree is mine," said the fairy. "Please don't cut it down."

Now the woodsman had never seen a tree fairy before, so he did not know what to make of it. "All right," he said. "If it's yours, then I won't cut it down."

"Thank you," said the tree fairy. "Now, since you have been so kind to me, I will grant you three wishes. Think before you use them, and use them wisely. Remember, no matter what they may be, your next three wishes will come true." Then the fairy disappeared.

The woodsman picked up his ax and started for
home. And as he walked, he thought about what he
should wish for.

When he got home, he told his wife what had
happened. Then *she* thought about what he should wish
for. Then they both sat down and *they* thought about
what he should wish for.

"I might wish for a bigger cottage," suggested the woodsman.

"No, not a cottage," said his wife. "A castle! With high towers and a wide drawbridge."

"I might wish for a bag full of gold," suggested the woodsman.

"Not a bag full," scolded his wife. "A barrel full! No ... a whole wagon full of gold."

"I could wish for a new cart," said the woodsman, " to haul my wood to market."

"No, not a cart," cried the wife. "A big, fancy coach! And a team of white horses to pull it along!"

"Just think of it!" said the woodsman. "We can have anything we want. And all we have to do is wish for it!"

"But we must be very careful," reminded his wife. "There is so much to ask for, and there are only three wishes. We must think and think and think until we are sure." So they thought and thought. And then they thought some more.

"All this thinking is making me hungry," said the woodsman. "Is supper ready yet?"

"Certainly not!" scolded his wife. "It is not yet suppertime, and supper will not be ready until it is time for supper!"

"That's too bad," said the woodsman, "because I'm
hungry right now. I wish I had some nice sausage to keep
my stomach from growling."

As soon as he had spoken, there came a noise from the chimney: *clatter, clatter, rustle, rustle!* And out came some sausage!

"Now look what you've done!" cried the wife. "You've wasted a wish!"

"So I have," agreed the woodsman. Then he said he was sorry, but his wife kept on scolding him.

"You fool!" she cried. "You wished for a sausage, when you could have had a whole pig! You could have had a whole farm, with hundreds of pigs!"

"I didn't think," said the woodsman.

"You never think!" cried the wife. "You wished for a sausage and wasted a wish! Now we have only two wishes left! What am I to do with you?"

"I'm sorry," said the woodsman again. He wanted his wife to be quiet. But his wife would not be quiet.

"No one but you would wish for a sausage!" she cried. "Now we must be even more careful than before. And it's all because of you! You didn't think. You wasted our first wish on a sausage!"

The woodsman did not want to listen to his wife any more. "Don't talk about the sausage," he said.

"Sausage! Sausage! Sausage!" she shouted.

Finally the woodsman could take no more. "I wish that sausage was stuck to your nose!" he cried. "Then maybe you wouldn't talk so much about it!"

At once, the sausage was stuck to the end of his wife's nose!

When he saw what had happened, the woodsman started to laugh. He couldn't help himself. "You look so funny with a sausage stuck to your nose!" he laughed.

"It's not funny!" wailed his wife. She tried to pull the sausage off her nose, but it was stuck. "Help me get it off!" she cried. But no matter how much they pulled and

tugged and tried to remove the sausage, it stayed where it was. The sausage was stuck to her nose and would not come off.

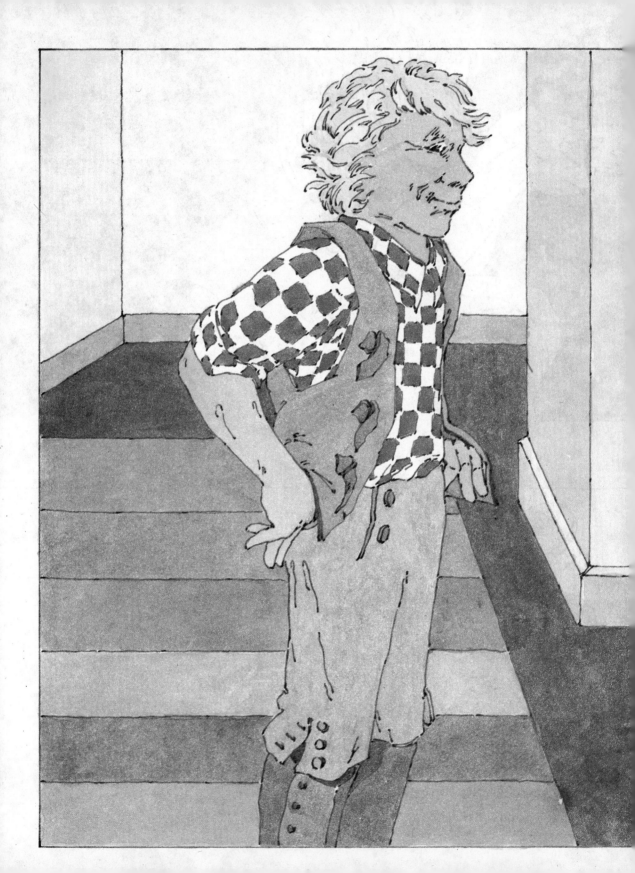

"Do something!" cried the woodsman's wife. She looked down at the sausage hanging from her nose.

The woodsman looked at the sausage, too. "I suppose I could get used to it," he said. "After all, not every man can say that his wife has a sausage hanging from her nose."

"Wish it off!" begged his wife. "You have one wish left."

"Ah, so I do!" exclaimed the woodsman. Then he sat down and pretended to forget about the sausage. "Now, let me think," he said. "What shall I use my last wish for? Shall I wish for jewels? Gold? Fancy clothes? A fine house?"

His wife stood silently and looked at him with sad, pleading eyes. It was the first time she had been silent in a long, long while.

"I wish ..." the woodsman said, "I wish that sausage would come off my wife's nose." And as soon as he had

made his wish, the sausage fell from his wife's nose onto the table.

And that was the last of the woodsman's three
wishes. He never had a bigger house, or a pile of gold.
And his wife never had fancy clothes or pretty jewelry.
But at least they had a fine sausage supper!